Farley & Breezy

By Kathy Adler
Illustrated by Doug Keith

Beachfront Books, LLC
Seattle, Washington

To Lisa and Cheryl…
With love from Mom

Library of Congress number 2005930076
ISBN 0-9768816-0-8

Published in the United States of America
by Beachfront Books, LLC
Seattle, Washington

Printed in Singapore by Tien Wah Press
Book Design: Molly Murrah, Murrah & Company, Kirkland, WA

 # Table of Contents

Chapter 1
Adventures

Farley Ferret lives with his
family in the woods near the
old farm.

"Be careful not to go near the
farmer," warns mother.

"No one will catch me,"

boasts Farley. "I'm too fast."

"You may be fast," wheezes Mother, "but the skunk's spray is faster. Hold still while I finish cleaning you."

"Aw mother. How was I supposed to know that skunks hide in old logs?" He weasels away from her constant licking. "Now Farley, you're not always fast enough." says mother. She puts her paw on his tail to keep him in place. "Remember what happened to you last month with that big dog?"

"I got away just in time," he says rubbing the tip of his tail.

"Next time, you may not be so lucky," grunts Mother.

Of course I'm lucky. And I'm fast. Mother doesn't know everything.

Chapter 2
Out To Lunch

Farley sees his sister, Breezy, sunning herself on a rock. He scampers over to her.

"Hey Breezy. Wanna play?"

"Not now, Farley. I'm busy." She bats a fly away from her nose.

"Come on, Breezy. I saw a rat nesting on the other side of the woods. Do you want to catch him with me?"

"A rat?" trills Breezy. "That sounds like a nice lunch. Are you fast enough, Farley?"

"Of course I am."

She slowly licks her lips. "Let's go."

Together they skitter through the underbrush and around clumps of trees.

Coming over a rise, Farley stops and looks down.

"Hey! Wait a minute, Farley. This is where the farmer lives. We're not supposed to be here."

"Relax, Breezy. We'll be in and out with the rat in a flash. Remember, I'm the fastest ferret in the woods."

"I'm not so sure about this."
Breezy sniffs the air. "That rat
does smell yummy."

"Okay. You stay here and keep
a look out for the farmer. I'll get
the rat."

Chapter 3
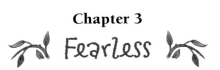 Fearless

Farley dashes down the hill.
He ducks under the low fence
and heads for the barn.

He peeks his head around
the corner of the doorway. The
farmer isn't there.

Standing on his hind legs he
sniffs the air for rat smells.

"Lovely," whispers Farley.

Breezy scurries across the yard to join him.

"I'm not staying out there by myself. And I'm sure not going in the barn."

"You wait here and I'll chase it out to you."

"Are you sure you're fast enough?"

"Not to worry. Just be ready to catch it when it runs your way."

Breezy sniffs the air. "I don't like this."

Farley slips quietly into the dark barn.

He turns around once to see Breezy peer around the doorway. The sunshine from outside helps him see as he hurries toward the rat smells.

Chapter 4
Rat Surprise

A minute ticks by. And then another. Farley keeps going past the horse stalls and nearer to the feed room.

There is a sudden movement in the feed room. Farley jerks his head up to see the rat. It runs past the farmer's feet.

"Ferret!" shouts the farmer.

"Skreek!" screams Farley.

"EEEK," screams the rat.

Farley turns and runs
straight into a pile
of empty cans.

CRASH!

Farley follows the rat towards the barn door with the farmer close behind.

The rat runs out.

Farley runs out.

Breezy gets ready to pounce.

Before she can move, Farley runs past the rat and keeps on running.

"Run, Breezy!" He squeals.

The farmer comes running out of the barn carrying a net on a pole.

He catches sight of Breezy.

She stares frozen to her spot.

The net comes down around her with a whoosh.

"Skreek!" she screams. "Farley! Help!"

Chapter 5
A Daring Rescue

Breezy's cries make Farley stop. He turns to see what has happened to his sister.

The farmer is bending over the net.

"Breezy," skreeks Farley.

Without thinking he turns and heads for the farmer. The farmer is walking back towards the barn carrying the net with Breezy in it.

When Farley is close enough he takes a flying leap. He lands on the farmer's back.

Farley bites down hard.

"AAGH," cries the farmer.

Farley hangs on and bites down again.

The farmer jumps straight up and twists hard. Farley flies across the yard.

The farmer takes off running.

Farley lays still.

Breezy scratches and claws her way out from under the net.

She rolls Farley over.

"Farley! Farley!"

Farley blinks then opens his eyes. He shakes his head to clear it and looks at Breezy.

"Let's get out of here," he squeals.

Chapter 6
The Fastest Ferret In The Woods

Together they run for the woods. Once there, they burrow under the roots of an old tree to catch their breath.

"You saved me from the farmer," wheezes Breezy. "You were so fast." She nuzzles him with her nose.

"Of course, I was," gasps Farley excitedly.

What if I couldn't save Breezy? he thinks to himself. I'd never see her again. Farley shivers.

He jumps up and looks straight at Breezy. "I'll never come here again," he cries.

"That's okay, Farley. Maybe you can chase something else."

"Like what?" asks Farley.

Breezy thinks a moment. "How about rabbits?"

"Yeah, rabbits," says Farley. He thinks about the rabbits that live across the meadow.

"I'm so tired, Farley." She rubs her eyes with her paws. "You can catch lunch for me tomorrow."

"And lunch tomorrow will be a fat rabbit, Breezy."

Together they head towards their home.

I know I'm faster than rabbits, thinks Farley.

Chapter 7
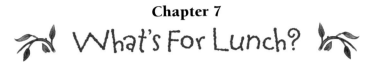 What's For Lunch?

The rain finally stops.

Water drips from the tree. The drops fall on Breezy's nose. She swipes at them with her paws.

"This rain is ruining my fur," wheezes Breezy.

"No it's not, Breezy. You look just the same as always."

"Brothers! What do they know about beauty?" She shakes her tail and sprays Farley.

"Stop it, Breezy. I was just trying to help." Farley dips his paws into a puddle of water and washes the mud from his toes.

Breezy rubs her head against the trunk of a tree. "If you want to help, find me something to eat. I'm starved."

"Me too," grunts Farley as he rolls over and over scratching his back.

"I've dreamed all morning of the rabbit you promised me," says Breezy. "I saw two rabbits across the meadow. Do you think you can catch one?"

"Yum," says Farley licking his lips. "I'm fast enough to catch any rabbit. Let's go."

They duck under the branches of a small tree and between two prickly bushes until they reach the path to the meadow.

Chapter 8
Rabbit Watch

"Slow down, Farley. Mud keeps getting stuck in my feet." Breezy waddles over to a log and thumps her paws against it. Mud flies everywhere.

"Where did you see the rabbits, Breezy?"

"Over there. They were near the edge of the meadow."

"Let's hide nearby and watch for them," says Farley.

"Where shall we hide, Farley?"
The meadow is open and wide.
The summer grasses are tall. But
they're not tall enough yet to hide
a ferret. The sun peeks out from
behind the clouds. Farley looks
around the edge of the meadow.
He sees a pile of rocks.

"We can hide on top of the rocks. Rabbits never look up."

Breezy looks up at the rocks. Then she notices a tall pine tree next to the rocks. "No. I think we should climb the tree," wheezes Breezy. "We can see further."

"Not me!" shrieks Farley.

"You can run faster, Farley. But I can climb better."

"Okay. You climb up in the tree and I'll hide on the rocks."

Farley scampers up to the top of the rocks.

Breezy climbs the tree.

"Rabbits look out," whispers Breezy as she reaches for another thick branch.

Chapter 9
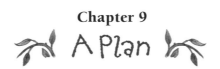 A Plan

"Farley. What do we do when we see a rabbit?" whispers Breezy.

"Hmmm," wheezes Farley. "We need a plan."

"Hmmm," sighs Breezy.

Sitting on their perches the gentle wind ruffles their fur.

They think and they think…

"I know," says Breezy. "When I see a rabbit, I'll run down the tree and chase it to you."

"Then the rabbit will hear you, Breezy."

"Okay. Then I'll drop a pine cone. You run around the rabbit and chase it to me."

"Good plan, Breezy."

They wait and wait…

The sun comes out. Farley can feel its warmth through the branches of the tree. He begins to feel sleepy. His head nods and his eyes begin to close.

Suddenly, a pine cone falls by Farley's paw.

Chapter 10
Catching Rabbits

Farley sees the rabbit hopping across the meadow. He slithers off the rock and quietly circles his prey. Breezy slips down the tree and hides in some bushes.

When the rabbit is almost across the meadow, Farley starts running towards it. He lets out a loud skreek as he runs.

The rabbit turns. When he sees Farley, he freezes.

Breezy sneaks out from behind the bushes and starts running.

Just as Farley and Breezy are about to catch him, he jumps straight up in the air. Farley and Breezy can't stop and run into each other. *Klunk!*

Rabbit comes down on top of them. He thumps them both with his strong back legs and races off into the woods.

Chapter 11
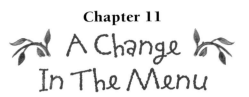
A Change In The Menu

Farley and Breezy lay there for a minute. Finally, Breezy sits up and rubs her head with muddy paws. "I'm a mess! My poor fur," she moans.

"Fur! My poor head," moans Farley. He stands up shaking mud and grass off of himself.

"I guess we're not having rabbit for lunch," sighs Breezy.

They slowly trot down to the stream for a quick bath. They tumble and roll in the cool, rushing water.

Farley climbs onto some low rocks to dry off. "Hey, Breezy. Are you still hungry?"

"Starving," says Breezy. She licks her fur until it shines.

"How does fish for lunch sound to you?"

Breezy sits up straight and looks at Farley. "Fantastic!"

They run back to the stream.
Standing in the shadows of a tree
they wait for lunch to float by.

Soon a fat trout swims by.
Farley and Breezy look at a each
other and lick their lips.

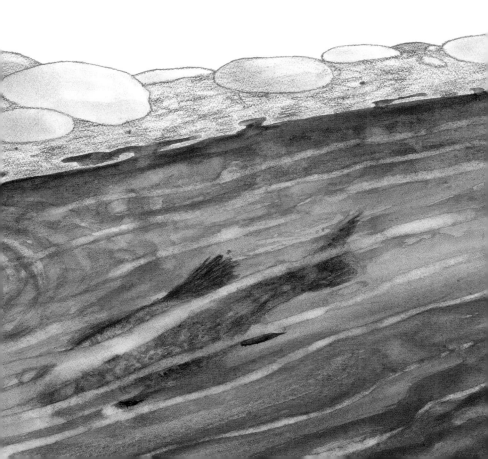

The end

Facts From Farley

Breezy and I are called Black Footed Ferrets. We are cousins of weasels, mink, otters and skunks.

Back in the 1850's, there were around one half million of us. We lived on the prairies of the Midwest. Prairie dogs were our main diet. When the farmers and ranchers settled in the Midwest they killed off the prairie dogs. Most of my family soon died off because there was no food.

In 1967 we were put on the endangered species list. By the year 1979 my family was declared extinct. In 1981 we fooled everyone. A farmer discovered a tiny population of us Black Footed ferrets near Meeteetse, Wyoming. So happy to see us, biologists started captive breeding programs.

Today, some of us live in conservation programs in several Midwest states. A small population of my family is also reported living freely and eating prairie dogs in Wyoming, South Dakota and Montana. We still remain on the endangered species list. So far, I'm still the fastest ferret!

You can learn more about my ferret family by visiting your school or local library.

 Farley's Questions

Why did I *not* pay attention to my mother's warning about the farmer?

Why did Breezy and I go to the farm?

What was Breezy supposed to do when we were at the barn?

Why did I tell Breezy to run?

What was the farmer going to do with Breezy?

What made me so brave?

Why does Breezy *not* like rain?

Why won't I climb a tree?

Can you think of a different plan to catch a rabbit?

Why did the rabbit freeze?

Am I fast enough to catch a fish?

Can you make up a story about Breezy and me?

About The Author

Kathy Adler loves animals of all kinds, except for snakes. Growing up she had dogs, fish and hamsters. She currently lives with a black lab named Maddie.

She loves to travel. When she visits South Pacific countries, she usually brings gifts of books to the local libraries of those countries. While visiting the Cook Islands in 1997, she met with the librarian there and saw the great need they had for children's books. She has been sending new and gently used children's books there every since. She has also been sending books to a friend in Tonga who shares the books with local children.

Kathy has always loved to write. It was her favorite subject in school. As an adult, she has been writing stories since her children were very young. *Farley & Breezy* is her first published book. She lives in Seattle Washington.

About The Illustrator

Doug Keith's background in commercial art, graphic design and fine art greatly influences his approach to picture book illustration, from story board to finished art. Such versatility earns Doug a wide range of projects, including more than forty illustrated books, a series of popular alphabet posters and numerous fine art commissions.

Among Doug's awards are a television Emmy for graphic design, The Society of Newspaper Design Award for illustration, and *ForeWord* magazine's 2004 Bronze Award for Best Picture Book of the Year, *The Errant Knight*.

Doug's sense of humor and ability to create personality in his characters worked quite well for *Farley & Breezy*. The wacky pair of ferrets can't seem to stay out of trouble and Doug captures this mischievous quality perfectly.

For this project, Doug used water color and colored pencil on illustration board.

Doug lives in north Seattle and commutes daily to his garage studio. To see more of his unique art, visit Doug's Web site: www.dougkeith.biz

Color Me Farley

Color Me Breezy